Is That For a *Boy* or a GIRL?

Written by S. Bear Bergman
Illustrated by Rachel Dougherty

Oh! Don't people have so many thoughts
About liking to dance or liking sports?
They say some things are for girls and some for boys:
Activities, clothes, colours and toys.
The shows on your TV? The stuff at the mall?
They make sure these ideas are heard by all.

Lots of kids don't fit in a box
(though you'd think we all did, the way most people talk).
So please meet my friends, with their own likes and ways
You might meet them - or be them! - one of these days.

I love bugs and crawly things.
Beetles and centipedes, creatures with wings—
T Rex and pterodon, all the dinos,
Lions, giraffes, tigers and rhinos.
But all the girls' clothes have the same two designs!
Just endless kittens and flowers on vines.
Where are my hot pink jungle cats?
My lavender raptors and glittery bats?

Sometimes I like my tiger pants,
And sometimes a spin-around dress.
There are days I adore my tidy braids,
But sometimes my hair is a mess.
People ask my folks a lot
"Is that a boy or a girl?"
My parents just smile and say
"That's Morgan,
The awesomest kid in the world!"

I don't know what I like yet.
I'm too little to choose, so whatever I get
Is picked by my family, my folks or their friends.
I get lots of presents (hope that never ends).

I know their search for awesome things is almost never done,
Not boy or girl or pink or blue, but green and orange; teaching and fun!
When they ask for help in a store,
The answer is SUCH a bore:
"Is that for a girl or a boy?

"Who cares? Show us only the coolest of toys!"

I love to play trains and busses and trucks.
That's just the way that I am.
But I'm also a kid who loves sparkle and shine,
And anything glitter or glam.
I've got lots of shirts in camo or black,
A train on the front, a truck on the back,
But my Dad's got a sackful of rhinestones and he
Outlines every last tractor in sparkles for me.

At Snack Queen I order a junior lunch.
Fish sandwich and apples, I like it a bunch.
Then they ask my Mom – "for a girl or a boy?"
How can I choose without seeing the toys?
Maybe it's robots, which I always like,
Or a little skateboard or tricky green bike.
But if it's an animal - especially a horse
Then that's the toy that I'll choose, of course.

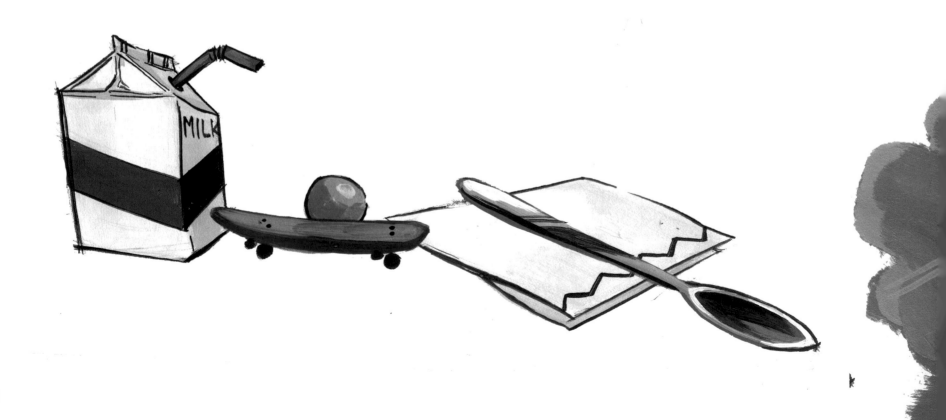

Dear person on the bus:

I'm not going to "sit like a lady."
I want to stretch and climb and bend, and
I have leggings on under my dress anyway.
My brother doesn't have to stop
Sucking his thumb, and it doesn't make him a "sissy"
no matter what you say.

Kids should do what makes them feel good.
Please mind your own business.

(I could rhyme if I felt like it, but I'm too cross.)

Monday is football, Wednesday's ballet,
Tuesday and Thursday I act in a play,

Sundays at church, Saturdays we bake,
Free time is reading (while I eat what I make).

I'll learn to snowboard next year when I'm tall
And shred down the mountain, big jumps but no falls.
I like to do everything; I mix all kinds of play!
My whole family does too, we're all happy that way.

I have a dress, just one, that I love,
With a sparkly skirt and some ruffles above.
Most days I like to wear sneakers and jeans,
But when I wear my dress, I know what that means—
I am airy and delicate, floating and prancing,
I twirl 'round my skirt and I cannot help dancing!
Tomorrow I'll go back to climb, jump, and run
But this fancy feeling is also such fun.

I'm sometimes a princess, I don't mind pink.
What bothers me more is the stuff people think.
My twin brother runs wild and it's "boys will be boys,"
I'm scolded if I even bang on my toys.
I'm powerful! I'm smart and I'm strong!
Don't look at me like I'm doing it wrong.
I could rescue myself from a dragon and tower.
My auntie says that I've got Girl Power.

Do I want to grow up to play basketball?
Did you ask just because I'm skinny and tall?
I like to play, but I love words and writing,
Also reading and reciting.
It's not "boyish", fast and tough,
But my words can be gentle or they can be rough.
I can tell real truths or make up worlds
Where sports and trucks are "only for girls."

At home I just use the bathroom.
There's no upset or drama or doom.
Like there is when I go to a store or to school,
And people act like I'm trying to fool
Them when I push open the right one for me.
They say I'm mistaken, how could that be?
I'm the expert, I'm in my own body.
Just let me pee! No need to get snotty.

For graduation, we make our procession
And celebrate all that we've done!
All the boys get a tie, girls get a rose,
They're forgotten as soon we're done with the show.

Everyone's asking me which one I'd wear.
That's awfully nice, and I'm so glad they care.
But why separate people by gender at all?
Just give us all hats, and let us stand tall.